"Horrid Henry is a fabulous antihe[...]
classic." —*Guardian*

"**Wonderfully appealing to girls** [...]
rarity at this age." —Judith Woods, *Times*

....

"The best children's comic writer."
—Amanda Craig, *Times*

....

"**I love the Horrid Henry books by Francesca Simon**.
They have lots of funny bits in. And Henry always gets into
trouble!" —Mia, age 6, *BBC Learning Is Fun*

"My two boys love this book, and **I have actually had tears
running down my face and had to stop reading because
of laughing so hard.**" —T. Franklin, Parent

"**It's easy to see why Horrid Henry is the bestselling
character for five- to eight-year-olds.**" —*Liverpool Echo*

"Francesca Simon's truly horrific little boy is **a
monstrously enjoyable creation.** Parents love them because
Henry makes their own little darlings seem like angels."
—*Guardian Children's Books Supplement*

"I have tried out the Horrid Henry books with groups of children as a parent, as a babysitter, and as a teacher. **Children
love to either hear them read aloud or to read them
themselves.**" —Danielle Hall, Teacher

"A flicker of recognition must pass through most teachers and parents when they read Horrid Henry. **There's a tiny bit of him in all of us**." —Nancy Astee, *Child Education*

"**As a teacher…it's great to get a series of books my class loves**. They go mad for Horrid Henry." —A teacher

"**Henry is a beguiling hero who has entranced millions of reluctant readers**." —*Herald*

....

"An absolutely fantastic series and surely a winner with all children. Long live Francesca Simon and her brilliant books! More, more please!" —A parent

....

"**Laugh-out-loud reading for both adults and children alike**." —A parent

"**Horrid Henry certainly lives up to his name, and his antics are everything you hope your own child will avoid—which is precisely why younger children so enjoy these tales**." —*Independent on Sunday*

"Henry might be unbelievably naughty, totally wicked, and utterly horrid, but **he is frequently credited with converting the most reluctant readers into enthusiastic ones**…superb in its simplicity." —*Liverpool Echo*

"Parents reading them aloud may be consoled to discover that Henry can always be relied upon to behave worse than any of their own offspring." —*Independent*

"**What is brilliant about the books is that Henry never does anything that is subversive.** She creates an aura of supreme naughtiness (of which children are in awe) but points out that he operates within a safe and secure world…**eminently readable** books." —Emily Turner, *Angels and Urchins*

"Accompanied by fantastic black-and-white drawings, the book is a joy to read. **Horrid Henry has an irresistible appeal to everyone—child and adult alike!** He is the child everyone is familiar with—irritating, annoying, but you still cannot help laughing when he gets into yet another scrape. Not quite a devil in disguise but you cannot help wondering at times! No wonder he is so popular!" —Angela Youngman

Horrid Henry by Francesca Simon

HORRID
HENRY
AND THE
MUMMY'S CURSE

Francesca Simon

Illustrated by Tony Ross

Jabberwocky
SOURCEBOOKS
AN IMPRINT OF SOURCEBOOKS

Text © Francesca Simon 2000
Internal illustrations © Tony Ross 2000
Cover illustrations © Tony Ross 2008
Cover and internal design © 2009 by Sourcebooks, Inc.

Published by Sourcebooks Jabberwocky, an imprint of Sourcebooks, Inc.
P.O. Box 4410, Naperville, Illinois 60567–4410
(630) 961–3900
Fax: (630) 961–2168
www.jabberwockykids.com

Originally published in Great Britain in 2000 by Orion Children's Books.

Library of Congress Cataloging-in-Publication Data

Simon, Francesca.
   Horrid Henry and the mummy's curse / Francesca Simon ; illustrated by Tony Ross.
      p. cm.
   Originally published: Great Britain : Orion Children's Books, 2000.
   [1. Behavior—Fiction.] I. Ross, Tony, ill. II. Title.
   PZ7.S604Hoaq 2009
   [Fic]—dc22
                              2008039688

Printed and bound in the United States of America.
VP 10 9 8 7 6 5 4 3

Source of Product: Versa Press, Inc. East Peoria, IL, USA
Date of Production: 12/17/09
Run Number: 11652

For my friends and advisers,
Joe and Freddy Gaminara

CONTENTS

1

HORRID HENRY'S HOBBY

"Out of my way, worm!" shrieked
Horrid Henry, pushing past his younger
brother Perfect Peter and dashing into
the kitchen.

"NO!" screamed Perfect Peter. He
scrambled after Henry and clutched
his leg.

"Get off me!" shouted Henry. He
grabbed the unopened Sweet Tweet
cereal box. "Nah nah ne nah nah,
I got it first."

Perfect Peter lunged for the Sweet
Tweet box and snatched it from Henry.
"But it's my turn!"

"No, mine!" shrieked Henry.

He ripped open the top and stuck his hand inside.

"It's mine!" shrieked Peter. He ripped open the bottom.

A small wrapped toy fell to the floor. Henry and Peter both lunged for it.

"Gimme that!" yelled Henry.

"But it's my turn to have it!" yelled Peter.

"Stop being horrid, Henry!" shouted Mom. "Now give me that thing!"

Henry and Peter both held on tight.

"NO!" screamed Henry and Peter. "IT'S MY TURN TO HAVE THE TOY!"

Horrid Henry and Perfect Peter both collected Gizmos from inside Sweet Tweet cereal boxes. So did everyone at their school. There were ten different colored Gizmos to collect, from the common green to the rare gold. Both Henry and Peter had Gizmos of every color. Except for one. Gold.

3

"Right," said Mom, "whose turn is it to get the toy?"

"MINE!" screamed Henry and Peter.

"He got the last one!" screeched Henry. "Remember—he opened the new box and got the blue Gizmo."

It was true that Perfect Peter had got the blue Gizmo—two boxes ago. But why should Peter get any? If he hadn't started collecting Gizmos to copy me, thought Henry resentfully, I'd get every single one.

"NO!" howled Peter. He burst into tears. "Henry opened the last box."

"Crybaby," jeered Henry.

"Stop it," said Peter.

"Stop it," mimicked Henry.

"Mom, Henry's teasing me," wailed Peter.

"I remember now," said Mom. "It's Peter's turn."

"Thank you, Mom," said Perfect Peter.

"It's not fair!" screamed Horrid Henry as Peter tore open the wrapping. There was a gold gleam.

"Oh my goodness," gasped Peter. "A gold Gizmo!"

Horrid Henry felt as if he'd been punched in the stomach. He stared at the glorious, glowing, golden Gizmo.

"It's not fair!" howled Henry. "I want a gold Gizmo!"

"I'm sorry, Henry," said Mom. "It'll be your turn next."

"But I want the gold one!" screamed Henry.

He leaped on Peter and yanked the Gizmo out of his hand. He was Hurricane Henry uprooting everything in his path.

"Helllllllllp!" howled Peter.

"Stop being horrid, Henry, or no more Gizmos for you!" shouted Mom. "Now clean up this mess and get dressed."

"NO!" howled Henry. He ran upstairs to his room, slamming the door behind him.

He had to have a gold Gizmo. He simply had to. No one at school had a gold one. Henry could see himself now, the center of attention, everyone pushing and shoving just to get a look at his gold Gizmo. Henry could charge 50¢ a peek. Everyone would want to see it and to hold it. Henry would be invited to every birthday party. Instead, Peter would be the star attraction. Henry gnashed his teeth just thinking about it.

But how could he get one? You couldn't buy Gizmos. You could only get them inside Sweet Tweet cereal boxes. Mom was so mean she made Henry and Peter finish the old box before she'd buy a new one. Henry had eaten mountains of Sweet Tweet cereal to collect all his Gizmos. All that hard work would be in vain, unless he got a gold one.

He could, of course, steal Peter's.

But Peter would be sure to notice, and Henry would be the chief suspect.

He could swap. Yes! He would offer Peter *two* greens! That was generous. In fact, that was really generous. But Peter hated doing swaps. For some reason he always thought Henry was trying to cheat him.

And then suddenly Henry had a brilliant, spectacular idea. True, it did involve a little tiny teensy weensy bit of trickery, but Henry's cause was just. *He'd* been collecting Gizmos far longer than Peter had. He deserved a gold one, and Peter didn't.

"So, you got a gold Gizmo," said Henry, popping into Peter's room. "I'm really sorry."

Perfect Peter looked up from polishing his Gizmos. "Why?" he said suspiciously. "*Everyone* wants a gold Gizmo."

Horrid Henry looked sadly at Perfect Peter. "Not anymore. They're very unlucky, you know. Every single person who's got one has died horribly."

Perfect Peter stared at Henry, then at his golden Gizmo.

"That's not true, Henry."

"Yes it is."

"No it isn't."

Horrid Henry walked slowly around Peter's room. Every so often he made a little note in a notebook.

"Marbles, check. Three knights, check. Nature kit—nah. Coin collection, check."

"What are you doing?" said Peter.

"Just looking at your stuff to see what I want when you're gone."

"Stop it!" said Peter. "You just made that up about gold Gizmos—didn't you?"

"No," said Henry. "It's in all the newspapers. There was the boy out walking his dog who fell into a pit of molten lava.

There was the girl who drowned in the toilet, and then that poor boy who—"

"I don't want to die," said Perfect Peter. He looked pale. "What am I going to do?"

Henry paused. "There's nothing you can do. Once you've got it you're sunk."

Peter jumped up.

"I'll throw it away!"

"That wouldn't work," said Henry. "You'd still be jinxed. There's only one way out—"

"What?" said Perfect Peter.

"If you give the gold away to someone brave enough to take it, then the jinx passes to them."

"But no one will take it from me!" wailed Peter.

"Tell you what," said Henry. "I'll take the risk."

"Are you sure?" said Peter.

"Of course," said Horrid Henry. "You're my brother. You'd risk your life for me."

"OK," said Peter. He handed Henry the gold Gizmo. "Thank you, Henry. You're the best brother in the world."

"I know," said Horrid Henry.

He actually had his very own gold
Gizmo in his hand. It was his, fair and
square. He couldn't wait to see Moody
Margaret's face when he waved it in
front of her. And Rude Ralph. He
would be green with envy.

Then Perfect Peter burst into tears
and ran downstairs.

"Mom!" he wailed. "Henry's going to
die! And it's all my fault."

"What?" screeched Mom.

Uh oh, thought Henry. He clutched
his treasure.

Mom stormed upstairs. She snatched
the gold Gizmo from Henry.

"How could you be so horrid,
Henry?" shouted Mom. "No TV for
a week! Poor Peter. Now get ready.
We're going shopping."

"NO!" howled Henry. "I'm not
going!"

★ ★ ★

Horrid Henry scowled as he followed
Mom up and down the aisles of the
Happy Shopper. He'd crashed the cart
into some people so Mom wouldn't let
him push it. Then she caught him
filling the cart with chips and soda and
made him put them all back. What a
horrible rotten day this had turned out
to be.

"Yum, cabbage," said Perfect Peter. "Could we get some?"

"Certainly," said Mom.

"And spinach, my favorite!" said Peter.

"Help yourself," said Mom.

"I want candy!" screamed Henry.

"No," said Mom.

"I want doughnuts!" screamed Henry.

"No!" screamed Mom.

"There's nothing to eat here!" shrieked Henry.

"Stop being horrid, Henry," hissed Mom. "Everyone's looking."

"I don't care."

"Well I do," said Mom. "Now make yourself useful. Go and get a box of Sweet Tweets."

"All right," said Henry. Now was his chance to escape. Before Mom could stop him he grabbed a cart and whizzed off.

"Watch out for the racing driver!" squealed Henry. Shoppers scattered as he zoomed down the aisle and screeched to a halt in front of the cereal section. There were the Sweet Tweets. A huge pile of them, in a display tower, under a twinkling sign saying, "A free Gizmo in every box! Collect them all!"

Henry reached for a box and put it in his cart.

And then Horrid Henry stopped.
What was the point of buying a whole
box if it just contained another green
Gizmo? Henry didn't think he could
bear it. I'll just check what's inside, he
thought. Then, if it *is* a green one, I'll be
prepared for the disappointment.

Carefully, he opened the box and
slipped his hand inside. Aha! There was
the toy. He lifted it out, and held it up
to the light. Rats! A green Gizmo, just
what he'd feared.

But wait. There was bound to be
a child out there longing for a green
Gizmo to complete his collection just
as much as Henry was longing for a
gold. Wouldn't it be selfish and horrid
of Henry to take a green he didn't need
when it would make someone else
so happy?

I'll just peek inside one more box,

thought Horrid Henry, replacing the box he'd opened and reaching for another.

Rip! He tore it open. Red.

Hmmm, thought Henry. Red is surplus to requirements.

Rip! Another box opened. Blue.

Rip! Rip! Rip!

Green! Green! Blue!

I'll just try one more at the back, thought Henry. He stood on tiptoe, and stretched as far as he could. His hand reached inside the box and grabbed hold of the toy.

The tower wobbled.

CRASH!

Horrid Henry sprawled on the ground. Henry was covered in Sweet Tweets. So was the floor. So were all the shoppers.

"HELP!" screamed the manager, skidding in the mess. "Whose horrid boy is this?"

There was a very long silence.

"Mine," whispered Mom.

★ ★ ★

Horrid Henry sat in the kitchen
surrounded by boxes and boxes and
boxes of Sweet Tweets. He'd be eating
Sweet Tweets for breakfast, lunch, and
dinner for weeks. But it was worth it,
thought Henry happily. Banned for life
from the Happy Shopper, how wonderful. He uncurled his hand to enjoy again
the glint of gold.

Although he *had* noticed that
Scrummy Yummies were offering a free
Twizzle card in every box. Hmmmm,
Twizzle cards.

2

....

HORRID HENRY'S HOMEWORK

Ahhhh, thought Horrid Henry. He turned on the TV and stretched out. School was over. What could be better than lying on the sofa all afternoon, eating chips and watching TV? Wasn't life great?

Then Mom came in. She did not look like a mom who thought life was grand. She looked like a mom on the warpath against boys who lay on sofas all afternoon, eating chips and watching TV.

"Get your feet off the sofa, Henry!" said Mom.

"Unh," grunted Henry.

"Stop getting chips everywhere!" snapped Mom.

"Unh," grunted Henry.

"Have you done your homework, Henry?" said Mom.

Henry didn't answer.

"HENRY!" shouted Mom.

"WHAT!" shouted Henry.

"Have you done your homework?"

"What homework?" said Henry. He kept his eyes glued to the TV.

"Go, Mutants!" he screeched.

"The five spelling words you are supposed to learn tonight," said Mom.

"Oh," said Henry. "*That* homework."

Horrid Henry hated homework. He had far better things to do with his precious time than learn how to spell "zipper" or work out the answer to 6 × 7. For weeks Henry's homework sheets had ended up in the recycling box until Dad found them. Henry swore he had no idea how they got there and blamed

22

Fluffy the cat, but since then Mom and Dad had checked his school bag every day.

Mom snatched the remote and switched off the TV.

"Hey, I'm watching!" said Henry.

"When are you going to do your homework, Henry?" said Mom.

"SOON!" screamed Henry. He'd just returned from a long, hard day at school. Couldn't he have any peace around here? When he was king anyone who said the word "homework" would get thrown to the crocodiles.

"I had a phone call today from Miss Battle-Axe," said Mom. "She said you got a zero in the last ten spelling tests."

"That's not *my* fault," said Henry. "First I lost the words, then I forgot, then I couldn't read my writing, then I copied the words wrong, then—"

"I don't want to hear any more silly excuses," said Mom. "Do you know your spelling words for tomorrow?"

"Yes," lied Henry.

"Where's the list?" Mom asked.

"I don't know," said Henry.

"Find it or no TV for a month," said Mom.

"It's not fair," muttered Henry, digging the crumpled spelling list out of his pocket.

Mom looked at it.

"There's going to be a test tomorrow," she said. "How do you spell 'goat'?"

"Don't you know how, Mom?" asked
Henry.

"Henry…" said Mom.

Henry scowled.

"I'm busy," moaned Henry. "I
promise I'll tell you right after Mutant
Madman. It's my favorite show."

"How do you spell 'goat'?" said Mom.

"G-O-T-E," snapped Henry.

"Wrong," said Mom. "What about
'boat'?"

"Why do I have to do this?" wailed
Henry.

"Because it's your homework," said
Mom. "You have to learn how to spell."

"But why?" said Henry. "I never
write letters."

"Because," said Mom. "Now spell
"boat."

"B-O-T-T-E," said Henry.

"No more TV until you do your
homework," said Mom.

"I've done all *my* homework," said
Perfect Peter. "In fact, I enjoyed it so
much I've already done tomorrow's
homework as well."

Henry pounced on Peter. He was
a cannibal tenderizing his victim for
the pot.

"Eeeeyowwwww!" screamed Peter.

"Henry! Go to your room!" shouted
Mom. "And don't come out until you
know *all* your spelling words!"

Horrid Henry stomped upstairs and

slammed his bedroom door. This was so unfair! He was far too busy to bother with stupid, boring, useless spelling. For instance, he hadn't read the new Mutant Madman comic book. He hadn't finished drawing that treasure map. And he hadn't even begun to organize his new collection of Twizzle cards. Homework would have to wait.

There was just one problem. Miss Battle-Axe had said that everyone who spelled all their words correctly tomorrow would get a pack of Big Bopper candy. Henry loved Big Bopper candy. Mom and Dad hardly ever let him have them. But why on earth did he have to learn spelling words to get some? If *he* were the teacher, he'd only give candy to children who couldn't spell. Henry sighed. He'd just have to sit down and learn those stupid words.

4:30. Mom burst into the room. Henry was lying on his bed reading a comic.

"Henry! Why aren't you doing your homework?" said Mom.

"I'll do it in a sec," said Henry. "I'm just finishing this page."

"Henry…" said Mom.

Henry put down the comic.

Mom left. Henry picked up the comic.

5:30. Dad burst into the room. Henry was playing with his knights.

"Henry! Why aren't you doing your homework?" said Dad.

"I'm tired!" yawned Henry. "I'm just taking a little break. It's hard having so much work!"

"Henry, you've only got five words to learn!" said Dad. "And you've just spent two hours *not* learning them."

"All right," snarled Henry. Slowly, he picked up his spelling list. Then he put it down again. He had to get in the mood. Soothing music, that's what he needed. Horrid Henry switched on his radio. The terrible sound of the Driller Cannibals boomed through the house.

"OH, I'M A CAN-CAN-CANNIBAL!" screamed Henry, stomping around his room. "DON'T CALL ME AN ANIMAL JUST 'CAUSE I'M A CAN-CAN-CANNIBAL!"

Mom and Dad stormed into Henry's bedroom and turned off the music.

"That's enough, Henry!" said Dad.

"DO YOUR HOMEWORK!" screamed Mom.

"IF YOU DON'T GET EVERY SINGLE WORD RIGHT IN YOUR TEST TOMORROW THERE

WILL BE NO TELEVISION FOR A
WEEK!" shouted Dad.

EEEK! No TV *and* no candy! This
was too much. Horrid Henry looked at
his spelling words with loathing.

GOAT

BOAT

SAID

STOAT

FRIEND

"I hate goats! I'll never need to spell
the word 'goat' in my life," said Henry.
He hated goat's cheese. He hated goat's
milk. He thought goats were smelly.

That was one word he'd definitely never need to know.

The next word was "boat." Who needs to spell that? thought Henry. I'm not going to be a sailor when I grow up. I get seasick. In fact, it's bad for my health to learn how to spell "boat."

As for "said," what did it matter if he spelled it "sed"? It was perfectly under-standable, written "sed." Only an old fusspot like Miss Battle-Axe would mind such a tiny mistake.

Then there was "stoat." What on earth was a stoat? What a mean, sneaky word. Henry wouldn't know a stoat if it sat on him. Of all the useless, horrible words, "stoat" was the worst. Trust his teacher, Miss Battle-Axe, to make him learn a horrible, useless word like stoat.

The last word was "friend." Well, a real friend like Rude Ralph didn't care how the word "friend" was spelled. As far as Henry was concerned any friend who minded how he spelled "friend" was no friend. Miss Battle-Axe included that word to torture him.

Five whole spelling words. It was too much. I'll never learn so many words, thought Henry. But what about tomorrow? He'd have to watch Moody Margaret and Jolly Josh and Clever Clare chomping away at those delicious Big Boppers, while he, Henry, had to gnash his empty teeth. Plus no TV for a week! Henry couldn't live that long without TV!

He was sunk. He was doomed to be candy-less, and TV-less.

But wait. What if there was a way to get that candy without the horrid hassle of learning to spell? Suddenly, Henry had a brilliant, spectacular idea. It was so simple Henry couldn't believe he'd never thought of it before.

He sat next to Clever Clare. Clare always knew the spelling words. All Henry had to do was to take a little peek at her work. If he positioned his chair right, he'd easily be able to see what she wrote. And he wouldn't be copying her, no way. Just double-checking. I am a genius, thought Horrid Henry. 100% right on the test. Loads of Big Bopper candy. Mom and Dad would be so thrilled they'd let him watch extra TV. Hurray!

Horrid Henry swaggered into class the

next morning. He sat down in his seat
between Clever Clare and Beefy Bert.
Carefully, he inched his chair over a
fraction so that he had a good view of
Clare's paper.

"Spelling test!" barked Miss Battle-
Axe. "First word—goat."

Clare bent over her paper. Henry
pretended he was staring at the wall,
then, quick as a flash, he glanced at her
work and wrote "goat."

"Boat," said Miss Battle-Axe. Again
Horrid Henry sneaked a look at Clare's
paper and copied her. And again. And again.

This is fantastic, thought Henry. I'll
never have to learn any spelling words.
Just think of all the comic books he could
read instead of wasting his time on homework! He sneaked a peek at Beefy Bert's
paper. Blank. Ha ha, thought Henry.

There was only one word left.
Henry could taste the tingly tang of a
Big Bopper already. Wouldn't he swag-
ger around! And no way would he share
his candy with anyone.

Suddenly, Clare shifted position and
edged away from him. Rats! Henry
couldn't see her paper anymore.

"Last word," boomed Miss Battle-Axe.
"Friend."

Henry twisted in his seat. He could
see the first four words. He just needed
to get a tiny bit closer…

Clare looked at him. Henry stared at
the ceiling. Clare glared, then looked

back at her paper. Quickly, Henry leaned over and...YES! He copied down the final word, "friend."

Victory!

Chomp! Chomp! Chomp! Mmmmm, boy, did those Big Boppers taste great!

Someone tapped him on the shoulder. It was Miss Battle-Axe. She was smiling at him with her great big yellow teeth.

Miss Battle-Axe had never smiled at
Henry before.

"Well, Henry," said Miss Battle-Axe.
"What an improvement! I'm thrilled."

"Thank you," said Henry modestly.

"In fact, you've done so well I'm
promoting you to the top spelling group.
Twenty-five extra words a night. Here's
the list."

Horrid Henry's jaws stopped
chomping. He looked in horror at the
new spelling list. It was littered with
words. But not just any words. Awful
words. Mean words. Long words.
HARD words.

Hieroglyphs.

Trapezium.

Diarrhea.

"AAAAAHHHHHHHHHHH!"
shrieked Horrid Henry.

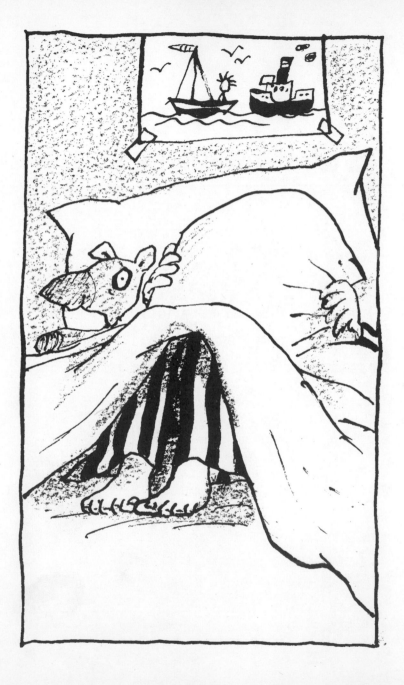

3

HORRID HENRY'S SWIMMING LESSON

Oh no! thought Horrid Henry. He pulled the blanket tightly over his head. It was Thursday. Horrible, horrible, Thursday. The worst day of the week. Horrid Henry was certain Thursdays came more often than any other day.

Thursday was his class swimming day. Henry had a nagging feeling that this Thursday was even worse than all the other awful Thursdays.

Horrid Henry liked the bus ride to the
pool. Horrid Henry liked doing the
dance of the seven towels in the changing room. He also liked hiding in the
lockers, throwing socks in the pool, and
splashing everyone.

The only thing Henry didn't like about going swimming was…swimming.

The truth was, Horrid Henry hated water. Ugggh! Water was so…wet! And soggy. The chlorine stung his eyes. He never knew what horrors might be lurking in the deep end. And the pool was so cold penguins could fly in for the winter.

Fortunately, Henry had a brilliant list of excuses. He'd pretend he had warts, or a tummy ache, or had lost his swimsuit. Unfortunately, the mean, nasty, horrible swimming teacher, Soggy Sid, usually made him get in the pool anyway.

Then Henry would duck Dizzy Dave, or splash Weepy William, or pinch Gorgeous Gurinder, until Sid ordered him out. It was not surprising that Horrid Henry had never managed to get his five-meter badge.

HORRID HENRY AND THE MUMMY'S CURSE

Arrrgh! Now he remembered. Today was test day. The terrible day when everyone had to show how far they could swim. Aerobic Al was going for gold. Moody Margaret was going for silver. The only ones who were still trying for their five-meter badges were Lazy Linda and Horrid Henry. Five whole meters! How could anyone swim such a vast distance?

If only they were tested on who could sink to the bottom of the pool the fastest, or splash the most, or spit water the farthest, then Horrid Henry would have every badge in a jiffy. But no. He had to leap into a freezing cold pool, and, if he survived that shock, somehow thrash his way across five whole meters without drowning.

Well, there was no way he was going to school today.

Mom came into his room.

"I can't go to school today, Mom," Henry moaned. "I feel terrible."

Mom didn't even look at him.

"Thursday itis again, I presume," said Mom.

"No way!" said Henry. "I didn't even know it was Thursday."

"Get up, Henry," said Mom. "You're going swimming and that's that."

Perfect Peter peeked around the door.

"It's badge day today!" he said. "I'm going for fifty meters!"

"That's great, Peter," said Mom. "I bet you're the best swimmer in your class."

Perfect Peter smiled modestly.

"I just try my best," he said. "Good luck with your five-meter badge, Henry," he added.

Horrid Henry growled and attacked.

He was a Venus flytrap slowly
mashing a frantic fly between his
deadly leaves.

"Eeeeeowwww!" screeched Peter.

"Stop being horrid, Henry!"
screamed Mom. "Leave your poor
brother alone!"

Horrid Henry let Peter go. If only
he could find some way not to take his
swimming test he'd be the happiest boy
in the world.

★ ★ ★

Henry's class arrived at the pool. Okay, thought Henry. Time to unpack his excuses to Soggy Sid.

"I can't go swimming, I've got a wart," lied Henry.

"Take off your sock," ordered Soggy Sid.

Rats, thought Henry.

"Maybe it's better now," said Henry.

"I thought so," said Sid.

Horrid Henry grabbed his stomach.

"Tummy pains!" he moaned. "I feel terrible."

"You seemed fine when you were prancing around the pool a moment ago," snapped Sid. "Now get changed."

Time for the killer excuse.

"I forgot my swimsuit!" said Henry. This was his best chance of success.

"No problem," said Soggy Sid. He handed Henry a bag. "Put on one of these."

Slowly, Horrid Henry rummaged in the bag. He pulled out a bikini top, a blue suit with a hole in the middle, a pair of pink underpants, a tiny pair of green trunks, a polka-dot one piece with bunnies, see-through white shorts, and a diaper.

"I can't wear any of these!" protested Horrid Henry.

"You can and you will, if I have to put them on you myself," snarled Sid.

Horrid Henry squeezed into the green trunks. He could barely breathe. Slowly, he joined the rest of his class pushing and shoving by the side of the pool.

Everyone had millions of badges sewn all over their suits. You couldn't even see Aerobic Al's bathing suit beneath the stack of badges.

"Hey you!" shouted Soggy Sid. He pointed at Weepy William. "Where's your swimsuit?"

Weepy William glanced down and burst into tears.

"Waaaaah," he wailed and ran weeping back to the changing room.

"Now get in!" ordered Soggy Sid.

"But I'll drown!" screamed Henry. "I can't swim!"

"Get in!" screamed Soggy Sid.

Good-bye, cruel world. Horrid Henry held his breath and fell into the icy water. ARRRRGH! He was turning into an iceberg!

He was dying! He was dead! His feet flailed madly as he sank down, down, down—clunk! Henry's feet touched the bottom.

Henry stood up, choking and spluttering. He was waist-deep in water.

"Linda and Henry! Swim five meters—now!"

What am I going to do? thought Henry. It was so humiliating not even being able to swim five meters! Everyone would tease him. And he'd have to listen to them bragging about their badges! Wouldn't it be great to get a badge? Somehow?

Lazy Linda set off, very very slowly. Horrid Henry grabbed onto her leg. Maybe she'll pull me across, he thought.

"Ugggh!" gurgled Lazy Linda.

"Leave her alone!" shouted Sid. "Last chance, Henry."

Horrid Henry ran along the pool's bottom and flapped his arms, pretending to swim.

"Did it!" said Henry.

Soggy Sid scowled.

"I said swim, not walk!" screamed Sid. "You've failed. Now get over to the far lane and practice. Remember, anyone who stops swimming during the test doesn't get a badge."

Horrid Henry stomped over to the far lane. No way was he going to practice! How he hated swimming! He watched the others splashing up and down, up and down. There was Aerobic Al, doing his laps like a bolt of lightning. And Moody Margaret. And Kung-Fu Kate. Everyone would be getting a badge but Henry. It was so unfair.

"Pssst, Susan," said Henry. "Have you heard? There's a shark in the deep end!"

"Oh yeah, right," said Sour Susan. She

looked at the dark water in the far end of
the pool.

"Don't believe me," said Henry.
"Find out the hard way. Come back
with a leg missing."

Sour Susan paused and whispered
something to Moody Margaret.

"Shut up, Henry," said Margaret.
They swam off.

"Don't worry about the shark,
Andrew," said Henry. "I think he's already
eaten today."

"What shark?" said Anxious Andrew.

Andrew stared at the deep end. It did
look awfully dark down there.

"Start swimming, Andrew!" shouted
Soggy Sid.

"I don't want to," said Andrew.

"Swim! Or I'll bite you myself!"
snarled Sid.

Andrew started swimming.

"Dave, Ralph, Clare, and Bert—start swimming!" bellowed Soggy Sid.

"Look out for the shark!" said Horrid Henry. He watched Aerobic Al tearing up and down the lane. "Gotta swim, gotta swim, gotta swim," muttered Al between strokes.

What a show-off, thought Henry. Wouldn't it be fun to play a trick on him?

Horrid Henry pretended he was a crocodile. He sneaked under the water to the middle of the pool and waited until Aerobic Al swam overhead. Then Horrid Henry reached up.

Pinch! Henry grabbed Al's thrashing leg.

"AAAARGGG!" screamed Al. "Something's grabbed my leg. Help!" Aerobic Al leaped out of the pool.

Tee hee, thought Horrid Henry.

"It's a shark!" screamed Sour Susan. She scrambled out of the pool.

"There's a shark in the pool!" screeched Anxious Andrew.

"There's a shark in the pool!" howled Rude Ralph.

Everyone was screaming and shouting and struggling to get out.

The only one left in the pool was Henry.

Shark!

Horrid Henry forgot there were no sharks in swimming pools.

Horrid Henry forgot *he'd* started the shark rumor.

Horrid Henry forgot he couldn't swim. All he knew was that he was alone in the pool—with a shark!

Horrid Henry swam for his life. Shaking and quaking, splashing and crashing, he torpedoed his way to the side of the pool and scrambled out.

He gasped and panted. Thank goodness.
Safe at last! He'd never ever go
swimming again.

"Five meters!" bellowed Soggy Sid.
"You've all failed your badges today,
except for—Henry!"

"Waaaaaaahhhhhh!" wailed the other
children.

"Whoopee!" screamed Henry.
"Olympics, here I come!"

4

HORRID HENRY
AND THE
MUMMY'S CURSE

Tiptoe. Tiptoe. Tiptoe.

Horrid Henry crept down the hall.
The coast was clear. Mom and Dad were
in the garden, and Peter was playing at
Tidy Ted's.

Tee hee, thought Henry, then darted
into Perfect Peter's room and shut the
door.

There it was. Sitting unopened on
Peter's shelf. The grossest, yuckiest, most
stomach-curdling kit Henry had ever
seen. A brand-new, deluxe "Curse of the
Mummy" kit, complete with a plastic
body to mummify, mummy-wrapping

gauze, curse book, amulets, and, best of all, removable mummy organs to put in a canopic jar. Peter had won it at the "Meet a Real Mummy" exhibition at the museum, but he'd never even played with it once.

Of course, Henry wasn't allowed into Peter's bedroom without permission. He was also not allowed to play with Peter's toys. This was so unfair, Henry could hardly believe it. True, he wouldn't let Peter touch his Boom-Boom Basher, his Goo-Shooter, or his Dungeon Drink kit. In fact, since Henry refused to share *any*

of his toys with Peter, Mom had forbid-
den Henry to play with any of Peter's
toys—or else.

Henry didn't care—Perfect Peter
had boring baby toys—that is, until he
brought home the mummy kit. Henry
had ached to play with it. And now was
his chance.

Horrid Henry tore off the wrapping
and opened the box.

WOW! So gross! Henry felt a delicious shiver. He loved mummies. What
could be more thrilling than looking at an
ancient, wrapped-up DEAD body? Even
a pretend one was wonderful. And now
he had hours of fun ahead of him.

Pitter-patter! Pitter-patter! Pitter-patter!

Oh help, someone was coming up the
stairs! Horrid Henry shoved the mummy
kit behind him as Peter's bedroom door
swung open and Perfect Peter strolled in.

"Out of my way, worm!" shouted
Henry.

Perfect Peter slunk off. Then he
stopped.

"Wait a minute," he said. "You're in
my room! You can't order me out of my
own room!"

"Oh yeah?" blustered Henry.

"Yeah!" said Peter.

"You're supposed to be at Ted's,"
said Henry, trying to distract him.

"He got sick," said Peter. He stepped
closer. "And you're playing with my kit!
You're not allowed to play with any of

my things! Mom said so! I'm going to tell her right now!"

Uh oh. If Peter told on him, Henry would be in big trouble. Very big trouble. Henry had to save himself, fast. He had two choices. He could leap on Peter and throttle him. Or he could use weasel words.

"I wasn't playing with it," said Henry smoothly. "I was trying to protect you."

"No you weren't," said Peter. "I'm telling."

"I was too," said Henry. "I was trying to protect you from the Mummy's Curse."

Perfect Peter headed for the door. Then he stopped.

"What curse?" said Peter.

"The curse that turns people into mummies!" said Henry desperately.

"There's no such thing," said Peter.

"Wanna bet?" said Henry. "Everyone knows about the mummy's curse! They take on the shape of someone familiar but really, they're mummies! They could be your cat—"

"Fluffy?" said Peter. "Fluffy, a mummy?"

Henry looked at fat Fluffy snoring peacefully on a cushion.

"Even Fluffy," said Henry. "Or Dad. Or Me. Or you."

"I'm not a mummy," said Peter.

"Or even—" Henry paused melo-dramatically and then whispered, "Mom."

"Mom, a mummy?" gasped Peter.

"Yup," said Henry. "But don't worry. You help me draw some Eyes of Horus. They'll protect us against…her."

"She's not a mummy," said Peter.

"That's what she wants us to think," whispered Henry. "It's all here in the mummy curse book." He waved the book in front of Peter. "Don't you think the mummy on the cover resembles you-know-who?"

"No," said Peter.

"Watch," said Horrid Henry. He grabbed a pencil.

"Don't draw on a book!" squeaked
Peter.

Henry ignored him and drew glasses
on the mummy.

"How about now?" he asked.

Peter stared. Was it his imagination or
did the mummy look a little familiar?

"I don't believe you," said Peter. "I'm
going straight down to ask Mom."

"But that's the worst thing you could
do!" shouted Henry.

"I don't care," said Peter. Down he went.

Henry was sunk. Mom would probably cancel his birthday party when Peter blabbed. And he'd never even had a chance to play with the mummy kit! It was so unfair.

Mom was reading on the sofa.

"Mom," said Peter, "Henry says you're a mummy."

Mom looked puzzled.

"Of course I'm a mummy," she said.

"What?" said Peter.

"I'm your mummy," said Mom, with a smile.

Peter took a step back.

"I don't want you to be a mummy," said Peter.

"But I am one," said Mom. "Now come and give me a hug."

"No!" said Peter.

"Let me wrap my arms around you," said Mom.

"NO WRAPPING!" squealed Peter. "I want my mommy!"

"But I'm your mummy," said Mom.

"I know!" squeaked Peter. "Keep away, you…Mummy!"

Perfect Peter staggered up the stairs to Henry.

"It's true," he gasped. "She said she was a mummy."

"She did?" said Henry.

"Yes," said Peter. "What are we going to do?"

"Don't worry, Peter," said Henry. "We can free her from the curse."

"How?" breathed Peter.

Horrid Henry pretended to consult the curse book.

"First we must sacrifice to the Egyptian gods Osiris and Hroth," said Henry.

"Sacrifice?" said Peter.

"They like cat guts, and stuff like that," said Henry.

"No!" squealed Peter. "Not…Fluffy!"

"However," said Henry, leafing through the curse book, "marbles are also acceptable as an offering."

Perfect Peter ran to his toy box and scooped up a handful of marbles.

"Now get me some toilet paper," added Henry.

"Toilet paper?" said Peter.

"Do not question the priest of Anubis!" shrieked Henry.

Perfect Peter got the toilet paper.

"We must wrap Fluffy in the sacred bandages," said Henry. "He will be our messenger between this world and the next."

"Meoww," said Fluffy, as he was wrapped from head to tail in toilet paper.

"Now you," said Henry.

"Me?" squeaked Peter.

"Yes," said Henry. "Do you want to free Mom from the mummy's curse?"

Peter nodded.

"Then you must stand still and be quiet for thirty minutes," said Henry. That should give him plenty of time to play with the mummy kit.

He started wrapping Peter. Round and round and round and round went the toilet paper until Peter was tightly wrapped from head to toe.

Henry stepped back to admire his
work. Goodness, he was a brilliant
mummy-maker! Maybe that's what he
should be when he grew up. Henry, the
Mummy-Maker. Henry, World's Finest
Mummy-Maker. Henry, Mummy-
Maker to the Stars. Yes, it certainly had
a ring to it.

"You're a fine-looking mummy, Peter," said Henry. "I'm sure you'll be made very welcome in the next world."

"Huuunh?"said Peter.

"Silence!" ordered Henry. "Don't move. Now I must utter the sacred spell. By the powers of Horus, Morus, Borus, and Stegosaurus," intoned Henry, making up all the Egyptian sounding names he could.

"Stegosaurus?" mumbled Peter.

"Whatever!" snapped Henry. "I call on the scarab! I call on Isis! Free Fluffy from the mummy's curse. Free Peter from the mummy's curse. Free Mom from the mummy's curse. Free— "

"What on earth is going on in here?" shrieked Mom, bursting through the door. "You horrid boy! What have you done to Peter? And what have you done to poor Fluffy?"

"Meoww," yowled Fluffy.

"Mommy!" squealed Perfect Peter.

Eowww, gross! thought Horrid Henry, opening up the plastic mummy body and placing the organs in the canopic jar.

The bad news was that Henry had been banned from watching TV for a week. The good news was that Perfect Peter had said he never wanted to see that horrible mummy kit again.

And now for a sneak peek at one of the
laugh-out-loud stories in
Horrid Henry Tricks and Treats

HORRID HENRY'S RAID

"You're such a pig, Susan!"

"No I'm not! You're the pig!"

"You are!" squealed Moody Margaret.

"You are!" squealed Sour Susan.

"Oink!"

"Oink!"

All was not well at Moody Margaret's Secret Club.

Sour Susan and Moody Margaret glared at each other inside the Secret Club tent. Moody Margaret waved the empty cookie tin in Susan's sour face.

"*Someone* ate all the cookies," said Moody Margaret. "And it wasn't me."

"Well, it wasn't me," said Susan.

"Liar!"

"Liar!"

Margaret stuck out her tongue at Susan.
Susan stuck out her tongue at Margaret.
Margaret yanked Susan's hair.

"Oww! You horrible meanie!"
shrieked Susan. "I hate you."

She yanked Margaret's hair.

"OWWW!" screeched Moody
Margaret. "How dare you?"

They scowled at each other.

"Wait a minute," said Margaret. "You
don't think—"

★ ★ ★

Not a million
miles away, sitting
on a throne inside
the Purple Hand
fort hidden behind
prickly branches,
Horrid Henry wiped
a few biscuit crumbs from his mouth and
burped. Mmmm boy, nothing beat the
taste of an archenemy's cookies.

The branches parted.

"Password!" hissed Horrid Henry.

"Smelly toads."

"Enter," said Henry.

The guard entered and gave the secret
handshake.

"Henry, why—" began Perfect Peter.

"Call me by my title, Worm!"

"Sorry, Henry—I mean Lord High
Excellent Majesty of the Purple Hand."

"That's better," said Henry. He waved
his hand and pointed at the ground. "Be
seated, Worm."

"Why am I Worm and you're Lord
High Excellent Majesty?"

"Because I'm the leader," said Henry.

"I want a better title," said Peter.

"All right," said the Lord High Excellent
Majesty, "you can be Lord Worm."

Peter considered.

"What about Lord High Worm?"

"OK," said Henry. Then he froze.

"Worm! Footsteps!"

Perfect Peter peeked through the leaves.

"Enemies approaching!" he warned.

Pounding feet paused outside the
entrance.

"Password!" said Horrid Henry.

"Dog poo breath," said Margaret,
bursting in. Sour Susan followed.

"That's not the password," said Henry.

"You can't come in," squeaked the
guard, a little late.

"You've been stealing the Secret Club
cookies," said Moody Margaret.

"Yeah, Henry," said Susan.

Horrid Henry stretched and yawned.

"Prove it."

Moody Margaret pointed to all the
crumbs lying on the dirt floor.

"Where did all these crumbs come
from, then?"

"Cookies," said Henry.

"So you admit it!" shrieked Margaret.

"Purple Hand cookies," said Henry.
He pointed to the Purple Hand skull

and crossbones
cookie tin.

"Liar, liar, pants
on fire," said
Margaret.

Horrid Henry
fell to the floor
and started rolling around.

"Ooh, ooh, my pants are on fire, I'm
burning, call the fire fighters!" shouted
Henry.

Perfect Peter dashed off.

"Mom!" he hollered. "Henry's pants
are on fire!"

Margaret and
Susan made a
hasty retreat.
Horrid
Henry stopped
rolling and
howled with
laughter.

"Ha ha ha ha ha—the Purple Hand rules!" he cackled.

"We'll get you for this, Henry," said Margaret.

"Yeah, yeah," said Henry.

"You didn't really steal their cookies, did you, Henry?" asked Lord High Worm the following day.

"As if," said Horrid Henry. "Now get back to your guard duty. Our enemies may be planning a revenge attack."

"Why do I always have to be the guard?" said Peter. "It's not fair."

"Whose club is this?" said Henry fiercely.

Peter's lip began to tremble.

"Yours," muttered Peter.

"So if you want to stay as a temporary member, you have to do what I say," said Henry.

"OK," said Peter.

"And remember, one day, if you're

very good, you'll be promoted from junior guard to chief guard," said Henry.

"Ooh," said Peter, brightening.

Business settled, Horrid Henry reached for the cookie tin. He'd saved five yummy chocolate fudge chewies for today.

Henry picked up the tin and stopped. Why wasn't it rattling? He shook it.

Silence.

Horrid Henry ripped off the lid and shrieked.

The Purple Hand cookie tin was empty. Except for one thing. A dagger drawn on a piece of paper. The dastardly mark of Margaret's Secret Club! Well, he'd show them who ruled.

"Worm!" he shrieked. "Get in here!"

Peter entered.

"We've been raided!" screamed Henry. "You're fired!"

"Waaaah!" wailed Peter.

★ ★ ★

"Good work, Susan," said the leader of the Secret Club, her face covered in chocolate.

"I don't see why you got three cookies and I only got two when I was the one who sneaked in and stole them," said Susan sourly.

"Tribute to your leader," said Moody Margaret.

"I still don't think it's fair," muttered Susan.

"Tough," said Margaret. "Now let's hear your spy report."

"NAH NAH NE NAH NAH!" screeched a voice from outside.

Susan and Margaret dashed out of the Secret Club tent. They were too late. There was Henry, prancing off, waving the Secret Club banner he'd stolen.

"Give that back, Henry!" screamed Margaret.

"Make me!" said Henry.

Susan chased him. Henry darted.
Margaret chased him. Henry dodged.

"Come and get me!" taunted Henry.

"All right," said Margaret. She walked
toward him, then suddenly jumped over
the wall into Henry's garden and ran to
the Purple Hand fort.

"Hey, get away from there!" shouted
Henry, chasing after her. Where was that
useless guard when you needed him?

Margaret nabbed Henry's skull and
crossbones flag and darted off.

The two leaders faced each other.

"Gimme my flag!" ordered Henry.

"Gimme my flag!" ordered Margaret.

"You first," said Henry.

"*You* first," said Margaret.

Neither moved.

"OK, at the count of three we'll throw them to each other," said Margaret.
One, two, three—throw!"

Margaret held on to Henry's flag.

Henry held on to Margaret's flag.

Several moments passed.

"Cheater," said Margaret.

"Cheater," said Henry.

"I don't know about you, but I have important spying work to get on with," said Margaret.

"So?" said Henry. "Get on with it. No one's stopping you."

"Drop my flag, Henry," said Margaret.

"No," said Henry.

"Fine," said Margaret. "Susan! Bring me the scissors."

Susan ran off.

"Peter!" shouted Henry. "Worm! Lord Worm! Lord High Worm!"

Peter stuck his head out of the upstairs window.

"Peter! Get the scissors! Quick!" ordered Henry.

"No," said Peter. "You fired me, remember?" And he slammed the window shut.

"You're dead, Peter," shouted Henry.

Sour Susan came back with the scissors and gave them to Margaret. Margaret held the scissors to Henry's flag. Henry didn't budge. She wouldn't dare—

Snip!

Aaargh! Moody Margaret cut off a corner of Henry's flag. She held the scissors poised to make another cut.

Horrid Henry had spent hours painting his beautiful flag. He knew when he was beat.

"Stop!" shrieked Henry.

He dropped Margaret's flag. Margaret dropped his flag. Slowly, they inched toward each other, then dashed to grab their own flag.

"Truce?" said Moody Margaret, beaming.
"Truce," said Horrid Henry, scowling.
I'll get her for this, thought Horrid
Henry. No one touches my flag and lives.

What tricks will Henry use to attack Margaret's fort?
Will Moody Margaret finally defeat Henry? Find out
whose flag is still waving at the end of the war in
Horrid Henry Tricks and Treats.

The HORRiD HENRY books
by Francesca Simon

Illustrated by Tony Ross
Each book contains four stories

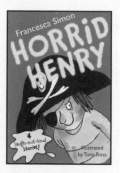

HORRID HENRY

Henry is dragged to dancing class against his will; vies with Moody Margaret to make the yuckiest Glop; goes camping; and tries to be good like Perfect Peter—but not for long.

HORRID HENRY TRICKS THE TOOTH FAIRY

Horrid Henry tries to trick the Tooth Fairy into giving him more money; sends Moody Margaret packing; causes his teachers to run screaming from school; and single-handedly wrecks a wedding.

HORRID HENRY and THE MEGA-MEAN TIME MACHINE

Horrid Henry reluctantly goes for a hike; builds a time machine and convinces Perfect Peter that boys wear dresses in the future; Perfect Peter plays one of the worst tricks ever on his brother; and Henry's aunt takes the family to a fancy restaurant, so his parents bribe him to behave.

HORRID HENRY'S STINKBOMB

Horrid Henry uses a stinkbomb as a toxic weapon in his long-running war with Moody Margaret; uses all his tricks to win the school reading competition; goes for a sleepover and retreats in horror when he finds that other people's houses aren't always as nice as his own; and has the joy of seeing Miss Battle-Axe in hot water with the principle when he knows it was all his fault.

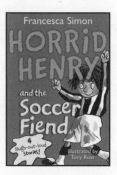

HORRID HENRY AND THE SOCCER FIEND

Horrid Henry reads Perfect Peter's diary and improves it; goes shopping with Mom and tries to make her buy him some really nice new sneakers; is horrified when his old enemy Bossy Bill turns up at school; and tries by any means, to win the class soccer match.

HORRID HENRY TRICKS AND TREATS

Horrid Henry encounters the worst babysitter in the world; traumatizes his parents on a long car trip; is banned from trick-or-treating at Halloween; and emerges victorious from a raid on Moody Margaret's Secret Club.

HORRID HENRY'S CHRISTMAS

Horrid Henry sabotages the Christmas play; tries to do all his Christmas shopping without spending any of his allowance; attempts to ambush Santa Claus (to get more presents of course); and has to endure the worst Christmas dinner ever!

About the Author

Francesca Simon spent her childhood on the beach in California and then went to Yale and Oxford Universities to study medieval history and literature. She now lives in London with her family. She has written over forty-five books and won the Children's Book of the Year in 2008 at the Galaxy British Book Awards for *Horrid Henry and the Abominable Snowman*.

Photo: Francesco Guidicini